THE LEGEND OF

Icebreaker

For a free color catalog describing Gareth Stevens' list of high-quality children's books, call 1-800-341-3569 (USA) or 1-800-461-9120 (Canada).

Library of Congress Cataloging-in-Publication Data

Westphal, Patricia Rae, 1958-
   The legend of Icebreaker / Patricia Rae Westphal.
      p. cm.
   Summary: An old man helps his fellow villagers find beauty and delight in the winter ice.
   ISBN 0-8368-0119-9
   [1. Folklore. 2. Winter—Folklore. 3. Ice—Folklore.] I. Title.
PZ8.1.W535Le 1991
398.23'6—dc20   89-40245

First published in the United States and Canada in 1991 by

Gareth Stevens Children's Books
1555 North RiverCenter Drive, Suite 201
Milwaukee, Wisconsin 53212, USA

This format copyright © 1991 by Gareth Stevens, Inc.
Text copyright © 1991 by Milwaukee Exposition and Convention Center and Arena (MECCA)

Designer: Laurie Shock

Printed in the United States of America

1 2 3 4 5 6 7 8 9 96 95 94 93 92 91

To my loving Mom and Dad
                       — Patti

With special love to my children,
Tracy and Scott
                       — Sally

THE LEGEND OF
Icebreaker

by
Patricia Rae Westphal

illustrated by
Sally Marinin

Gareth Stevens Children's Books
MILWAUKEE

Years before history was
recorded a tale became
a legend, and this is how
it began.

By the gathering of waters the seasons changed. The summers were short and glorious, but the winters were long, and few ventured from their homes. The families in the village were quite content to busy themselves in their winter shelters.

On their brief outings the men, and the women, and the children kept their eyes and minds to the tasks at hand: gathering firewood, fishing through the ice, hunting for food, not resting until they were again inside their dark homes, by their dull red fires.

But next to the frozen waters lived an old man named Isa. And with Isa lived memories from his childhood: memories of a time when his friends and his family had celebrated the ice-cold season. They loved the long festival of winter, and the beauty of the snow-covered forests.

How Isa longed to see children playing, parents laughing, and one friend meeting another to enjoy the sun's reflections off the crystal glaciers.

9

Isa would look from his window and see the beauty. He dreamed of stirring the village to take part in it. So one day, as the villagers scurried doggedly about their tasks, Isa ventured out and climbed to the top of an ice peak, close by the huddled huts. He paused, breathing heavily from the climb, and as he recovered, inspiration from the stark beauty around him flooded into his lungs.

Isa called out, "This is the place to gather. Bring your children and we will enjoy this time together." But to his dismay, no one looked up, no one came.

He stood for a few minutes, and sadness filled his heart. Slowly, Isa walked down from the ice peak. Suddenly a scene swam before his eyes and he felt giddy, and sank to his knees. And as the giddiness left him, he noticed something glinting within the ice. A buried container, a capsule of some kind! Yes, but there was something unusual about it.

Isa's heart jumped with happiness at his discovery. This container was truly different. It had taken on a glow of its own, and Isa could see that something was inside the mysterious capsule, something that looked like . . . an animal! The glow shimmered. Did the shape move? Could it be alive?

Night was approaching, and Isa had nothing to dig with, so he rose to his feet and continued home, pondering on the capsule. Why was it there? How did it get there? Tomorrow I will remove it, Isa thought.

That night the wind blew so hard that it whistled and the candlelight flickered. A warm excitement blazed within Isa, and he fell into a deep sleep. He began to dream, and this was how he dreamed.

In the darkness a vapor rose from the window ledge, causing a hoarfrost. The frost produced designs that appeared ornamental and continued to change. Within his dream, the hoarfrost vapor began to speak: "Find a light, and there you will find the Sundog. Find the Sundog, and you will bring happiness and laughter to your people."

Isa was frightened by the voice and also confused, but he fell back into a deep sleep.

The next morning, Isa woke and found detailed patterns of castles, children, and crystals on the window where the vapor had appeared the night before. Isa also noticed a glow of light shining through the patterns. It seemed to beckon him. He went to the window, scratched some of the frost away, and found that this sunlike reflection was coming from the ice peak where he had stood the day before.

Isa scrambled into his big old pants, pulled on his boots, tied a thick belt around his waist, slipped on his heavy wool coat, and ran to the shed.

He chose a pick and a shovel and other tools that he thought he might need. As he approached the ice peak the mysterious capsule grew brighter and brighter. It was so bright that he had to squint as he stood at the spot beneath which the glowing capsule lay. With a fervor and energy amazing for a man his age he began to wedge his way into the glowing ice.

As Isa worked at the ice he thought about the vapor the night before. Was it really a dream? Is this really happening?

Isa continued to work away at the ice but soon discovered that his project was going to take longer than he had anticipated. Each time Isa was ready to reach down and remove the glowing container, it would magically recede and move to another area of the ice peak. But instead of turning back, Isa found that his energy and resolve doubled each time this happened, and he worked until night fell.

Day after day Isa returned, feeling more and more energized by his undertaking. He welcomed each movement of the magical container. And with each movement, Isa would laugh, twirl around in a dance, and sing out, "You moved again, you little Sundog."

Meanwhile, the villagers grew curious about Isa's furious activity on the ice peak. Soon they grew so perplexed that they gathered below the ice peak. Then one of the children shouted, "Hey, Icebreaker, why are you carving that castle in the ice?"

23

Isa the Icebreaker turned to
the child with a warm smile,
but also with a look of
puzzlement in his eyes. He
put down his tools and
stepped down to where the
people were gathered. He
took the child's hand and
looked up.

Icebreaker finally saw that he
had carved a beautiful castle
glistening with radiant crystals.
And then, within a blink of an
eye, a puff of vapor filled the
doorway to the castle.

When the vapor lifted, there stood the Sundog. One of a kind. He bounded and barked happily in and out of the crowd, infecting the people with good humor. The children began to run around the castle and play. They ran to find rocks and carving sticks, and happily began to build with the snow and carve play shapes out of the mountains of ice by the lakeside.

More and more people gathered together, and soon the whole village was celebrating the Icebreaker's dream. Fathers and mothers, young men and women, and children all saw what a beautiful winter world they lived in. The festivities and celebrating lasted well into the night.

In the morning there was no
sign of the Sundog and Isa the
Icebreaker was nowhere to be
seen. The villagers searched
the lakeshore, the riverbanks,
the forest. The Sundog and
Isa were gone, but they left
behind a spark in the hearts
of each one of the villagers, a
bright feeling of fun and
wonder, and a lively sense
of the gifts that their long
winters bring.

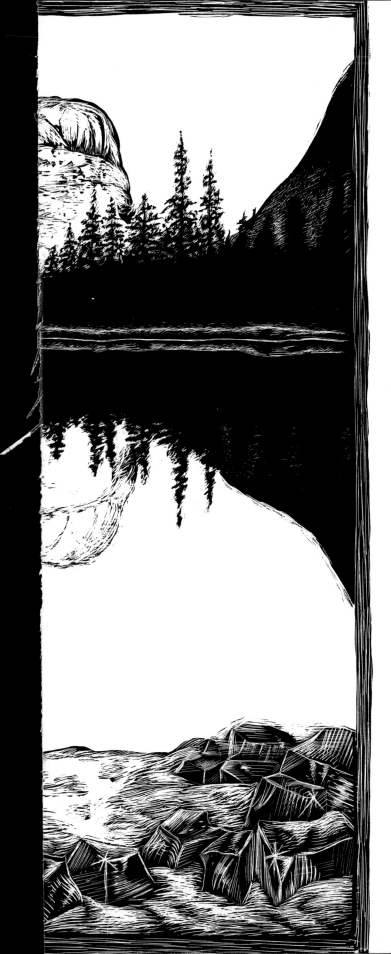

And each year, when the winter blows so cold that the ice floes on the lake pile up against the lakeshore, Icebreaker returns with Sundog to carve wondrous and magical shapes in the ice. And if you go down to the lake on one of these sparkling days, you can tell if they have been there.

In the vast, jagged ice-scape
and among the ice peaks,
you can see the castles, huts,
and frozen fires, the faces of
happy children and older
village people from those first
days of long ago.